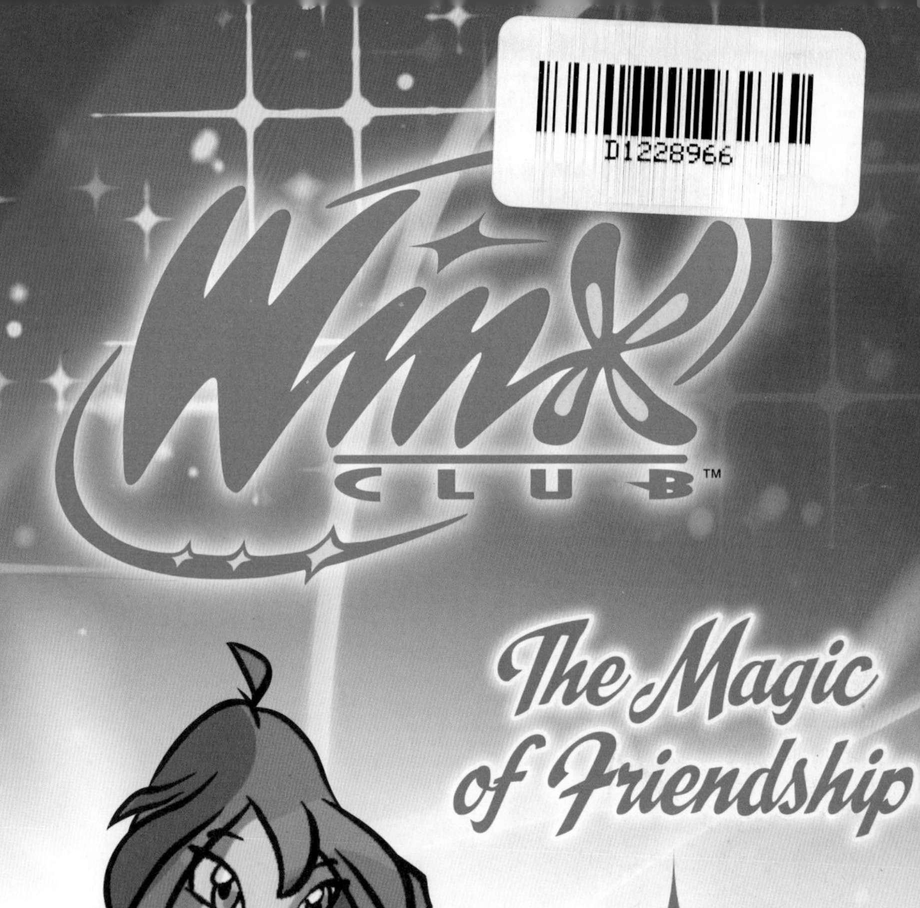

The Magic of Friendship

3

As seen on nickelodeon

Winx Club
Volume 3

Designer • Fawn Lau
Letterer • Susan Daigle-Leach
Adaptation • Ysabet MacFarlane
Editor • Amy Yu

Printed in China

Published by VIZ Media, LLC
P.O. Box 77010
San Francisco, CA 94107

10 9 8 7 6 5 4 3 2 1
First printing, September 2012

nickelodeon

www.vizkids.com

www.viz.com

Table of Contents

Volume 3

Meet the Winx Club

Bloom

Raised on Earth, **BLOOM** had no idea she had magical fairy powers until a chance encounter with Stella. Intelligent and loyal, she is the heart and soul of the Winx Club.

A princess from Solaria, **STELLA** draws her fairy power from sunlight. Optimistic and carefree, she introduces Bloom to the world of Magix.

Self-confident and a perfectionist, **TECNA** has a vast knowledge of science, which enables her to create devices that can get her and her friends out of trouble.

MUSA draws power from the music she plays. She has a natural talent for investigating, and she's got a keen eye for details.

FLORA draws her fairy powers from flowers, plants and nature in general. Sweet and thoughtful, she tends to be the peacemaker in the group.

Their Friends

The Specialists

Riven

Timmy

Sky

Brandon

These boys from Red Fountain School are friends with the Winx Club girls and sometimes team up with them to fight trolls and other magical monsters.

Their Foes

THE TRIX are an evil trio of witches from Cloudtower Academy who battle the Winx Club regularly. With leader Icy's freezing powers, Stormy's weather-controlling powers, and Darcy's powers of darkness, these girls love to wreak havoc!

Stormy

Icy

Darcy

A Job for Bloom

BLOOM'S ADVENTURES AT ALFEA SCHOOL FOR FAIRIES CONTINUE, BUT IT LOOKS LIKE SHE'LL NEED TO GET A JOB IN ORDER TO STAY IN MAGIX! MEANWHILE, STELLA IS ABOUT TO GIVE BLOOM AN AMAZING PRESENT...
BLOOM, I HAVE A GIFT FOR YOU!
FOR ME?
I WANTED TO GET YOU SOMETHING SPECIAL–TO THANK YOU FOR BEING SUCH A GOOD FRIEND.
STELLA, YOU DIDN'T HAVE TO DO THAT!
BEING FRIENDS WITH YOU AND THE REST OF THE WINX CLUB GIRLS IS SPECIAL ENOUGH!
YEAH, BUT I REALLY WANTED TO DO THIS! I MEAN, YOU'VE SAVED MY LIFE A COUPLE OF TIMES NOW, YOU KNOW!
GO ON, OPEN IT! I WANNA SEE IF YOU LIKE IT!
OKAY, OKAY! LOOKS LIKE KIKO'S CURIOUS, TOO!
OH, IT'S A DIARY! WOW... IT'S BEAUTIFUL!
KIIII!

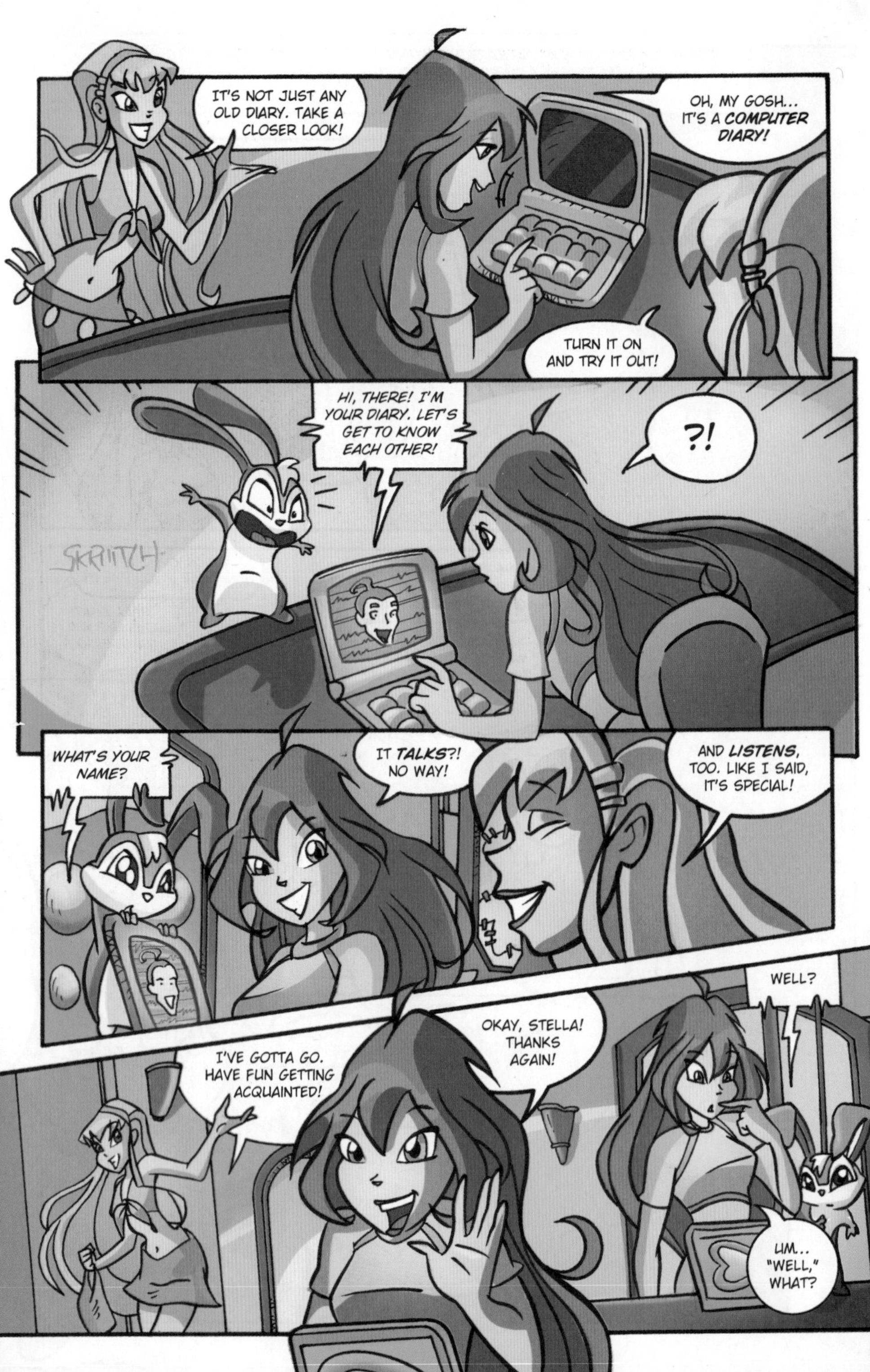
IT'S NOT JUST ANY OLD DIARY. TAKE A CLOSER LOOK!
OH, MY GOSH... IT'S A COMPUTER DIARY!
TURN IT ON AND TRY IT OUT!
HI, THERE! I'M YOUR DIARY. LET'S GET TO KNOW EACH OTHER!
?!
SKRIITCH
WHAT'S YOUR NAME?
IT TALKS?! NO WAY!
AND LISTENS, TOO. LIKE I SAID, IT'S SPECIAL!
I'VE GOTTA GO. HAVE FUN GETTING ACQUAINTED!
OKAY, STELLA! THANKS AGAIN!
WELL?
UM... "WELL," WHAT?

KNOWING YOUR NAME IS MY FIRST STEP TO KNOWING YOU! I WON'T REALLY BE YOUR DIARY UNTIL YOU TELL ME.
OH! I... WELL, I...
MAYBE YOU DON'T LIKE HOW I LOOK? I CAN BE ANYTHING YOU WANT! MAYBE A WISE OLD GRANDFATHER?
OR MAYBE A WITTY, PRETTY NEW FRIEND?
MAYBE A CUTE CARTOON CHARACTER?
NOOO, THAT'S OKAY. LET'S GO WITH THE FIRST LOOK!
GOOD CALL! I PREFER THE SERIOUS LOOK MYSELF. NOW, WHERE WERE WE?
YOU ASKED FOR MY NAME. IT'S BLOOM!
GREAT! NOW THAT YOU'VE TOLD ME, NO ONE ELSE CAN SWITCH ME ON AND TALK TO ME!
YOU CAN SHARE ANY SECRET. I WON'T TELL A SOUL.
REALLY?

GIVE IT A TRY! CONFIDE IN ME! I'M ALL EARS.
HMM... LIKE WHAT? I CAN'T THINK OF ANY...
HOW DO YOU KNOW THAT? WHO TOLD YOU?
YOU COULD START WITH THIS CUTE GUY. HE MEANS A LOT TO YOU, DOESN'T HE?
WHAT?!
STELLA, NATURALLY. WE HAD A NIIICE LITTLE HEART-TO-HEART WHEN SHE BOUGHT ME!
SHE TOLD ME ABOUT ALFEA, THE WINX CLUB, THE BOYS... I'M A CURIOUS DIARY!
HMPH! I THINK YOU MEAN "GOSSIPY"!
HEY, WHAT'S THE HARM? IT'S ALL PART OF BEING A DIARY! AND LIKE I SAID–I KEEP ALL YOUR SECRETS!
SO IF SKY IS YOUR BOYFRIEND, I'LL FILE THAT FACT SAFELY AWAY.
WELL, HE'S NOT MY BOYFRIEND. NOT YET, ANYWAY!
SO HE DOESN'T KNOW HOW YOU FEEL?
WELL, HE'S GREAT, BUT THERE'S SOMETHING MYSTERIOUS ABOUT HIM.

A SECRET AT LAST! TELL ME MORE!
OH, I DON'T WANT TO TALK ABOUT HIM RIGHT NOW. I'VE GOT OTHER THINGS ON MY MIND!
FRANKLY, I'M WORRIED ABOUT MONEY. I'M ALMOST BROKE!
OH, NO! IF YOU CAN'T PAY FOR SCHOOL, THEY'LL TOSS YOU OUT!
"IT'S NOT THAT BAD, THANK GOODNESS. HEADMISTRESS FARAGONDA CALLED ME INTO HER OFFICE A FEW DAYS AGO..."
YOU'RE OUR ONLY STUDENT FROM EARTH, AND YOU'VE BEEN GETTING GOOD GRADES, SO WE'RE GIVING YOU A SCHOLARSHIP!
SO I DON'T HAVE TO WORRY ABOUT TUITION, BUT I STILL HAVE DAY-TO-DAY EXPENSES.
HMM... WHAT DO YOUR FRIENDS SAY?
THEY DON'T REALLY UNDERSTAND WHAT IT'S LIKE. STELLA AND TECNA COME FROM RICH FAMILIES, SO THEY'RE ALL SET. FLORA CAN COUNT ON HER FOLKS, TOO...
BUT MUSA AND I HAVE THIS SAME PROBLEM, SO WE'VE BOTH DECIDED TO FIND JOBS.
WHAT KIND OF JOBS?
HAVEN'T FIGURED THAT PART OUT YET! IT WON'T BE EASY, BUT WITH ANY LUCK...

"...HARD WORK WILL GET US TO NEW PLACES!"
BOOM! CRASH!
WHAT'S THE MEANING OF ALL THIS?
THIS IS A LIBRARY! KEEP THE NOISE DOWN!
BUT WE'RE WORKING, MA'AM. WE CAN'T BE ANY QUIETER!
BESIDES, LOOK WHO'S TALKING! YOU'RE SHOUTING YOURSELF.
I-I WAS BEING EMPHATIC! IT'S NOT THE SAME AT ALL!
WE WERE JUST TRYING TO REPAIR THE WALL, AND IT COLLAPSED. IT'S ALL EMPTY SPACE BACK THERE!
WHAT? BUT THERE SHOULDN'T BE...!

OH, MY GOODNESS. THERE'S A WHOLE ROOM HERE!
AND IT'S FAR FROM EMPTY! BRING ME A LIGHT!
THERE ARE BOOKS EVERYWHERE! THEY MUST HAVE BEEN STORED AWAY AND FORGOTTEN FOR YEARS.
WE'LL HAVE TO CLEAN THEM UP, CLASSIFY THEM, ORGANIZE THEM... AS IF I'M NOT BUSY ENOUGH! I'LL NEVER GET THIS DONE WITHOUT HELP!
!
EXCUSE ME... MISS BARBATEA? I HAVE AN IDEA...

SOON...
GUESS WHAT, WINX CLUB? YOU'RE LOOKING AT A GIRL WITH A SHINY NEW JOB!
HUH?
A JOB? WHERE, MUSA?
AT THE LIBRARY!
REALLY? COOL!
THEY FOUND A ROOM IN THE BASEMENT WITH HEAPS OF OLD BOOKS. MISS BARBATEA TOOK ONE LOOK AT THE MESS AND FREAKED OUT...
...SO WHEN I OFFERED TO HELP, SHE HIRED ME ON THE SPOT!
SHE DID? AND SHE'S GONNA PAY YOU?

OF COURSE SHE IS! IT WON'T BE MUCH, BUT IT'S ONLY FIVE HOURS A WEEK. IT'S PERFECT FOR ME!
LUCKY YOU!
WHAT KIND OF BOOKS DID THEY FIND?
A BUNCH OF OLD MANUSCRIPTS, PLUS SOME MUSIC SCORES! THAT'S WHY I'M PERFECT FOR THE JOB!
IT'LL BE SO EXCITING TO DECIPHER THOSE OLD MELODIES AND PLAY THEM. I CAN'T WAIT TO GET STARTED!
THAT'S AWESOME, MUSA! I'M SO HAPPY FOR YOU!
SIGH... I CAN'T WAIT TO FIND A JOB OF MY ***OWN***...
OH, BLOOM, DO YOU REALLY HAVE TO? IF YOU WANT, I COULD LOAN YOU MONEY—
STOP RIGHT THERE, STELLA. I APPRECIATE THAT, BUT YOU ALREADY GAVE ME A WONDERFUL GIFT. I'LL TAKE CARE OF THIS MYSELF.
I'VE MADE A LIST OF POSSIBILITIES...AND AFTER CLASS TOMORROW, I'LL START CHECKING THEM OUT.

UGH!
RAIN, RAIN, GO AWAY...
PRRrrrrRT!
NOT THE BEST DAY FOR JOB-HUNTING, BUT I CAN'T PUT IT OFF ANY LONGER. I'LL START WITH THE TOP OF MY LIST...
FIRST UP, THE FLOWER SHOP! I HAVE PLENTY OF EXPERIENCE FROM WORKING IN MOM'S SHOP...

..."I'M SURE THEY'LL HIRE ME!"
WE DON'T REQUIRE ANY SALES STAFF. WE'RE DOING QUITE WELL FOR OURSELVES.
I'M SURE YOU ARE! BUT MAYBE ON THE WEEKEND, WHEN THERE'RE LOTS OF PEOPLE...
THERE ARE NEVER LOTS OF PEOPLE HERE! WE HAVE A VERY SELECT CLIENTELE!
OOOOH, A "SELECT CLIENTELE"! LA-DEE-DAH!
I WOULDN'T SHOP THERE IF I WERE YOU. THEY MIGHT THINK YOU'RE NOT GOOD ENOUGH TO SELECT!
?!
UGH! THE NEXT STORE'S ALL THE WAY ACROSS TOWN... BUT MAYBE I'LL HAVE BETTER LUCK THERE!

SORRY, MY DEAR, BUT I DON'T NEED A SALESGIRL. THERE'S BARELY ENOUGH WORK FOR ME AS IT IS!
WHY DON'T YOU TRY THE SUPERMARKET ACROSS THE STREET? MAYBE THEY'LL HIRE YOU!
THANKS!
BUT NO LUCK THERE...
A FEW HOURS A DAY? NO! HERE, WE WORK MORNING TO NIGHT!
...AND NONE AT THE BAKERY ON THE CORNER, EITHER...
I CAN'T HIRE A STUDENT WHO CAN'T WORK MORNINGS. BUT HERE—HAVE A CUPCAKE!
NOT EVEN AT "MAGIX COSMETICS," THE CHIC MAKEUP STORE IN TOWN!
YOU'RE FAR TOO YOUNG! WE SELL PERFUME, NOT TOYS!
THANKS, ANYWAY! HMPH.

AAAAAH-CHOOO!
NOW, CLASS... LET'S SEE HOW THESE VARIOUS SUBSTANCES CAN CHANGE THE PROCESS OF TRANSFORMATION!
WE CAN DIVIDE THEM INTO THREE MAIN CATEGORIES: SWEET, BITTER AND—
AAAAH-CHOOO!
BLOOM, IF YOU CONTINUE TO SNEEZE, WE'LL NEVER GET ANYTHING DONE! YOU'RE DISTRACTING THE WHOLE CLASS—AND WORSE, DISTRACTING *ME*!
SNIFF! I'M SORRY, PROFESSOR WIZGIZ!
I GOT SOAKED IN THE RAIN YESTERDAY, AND... *AAAAAH...*
WAIT! DON'T—

...CHOOO!!
OHH!
VOOOOSH
KRASH
CLINK
OH, NO! NOT THE RED CABBAGE INFUSION! I'M ALLERGIC TO CABBAGE—
POOF
OOOH!
IT ALWAYS TRANSFORMS ME INTO SOMETHING VILE! SEE? IT HAPPENED AGAIN.
I HOPE YOU HAVE A STRONG STOMACH, MISS BLOOM, BECAUSE NOW YOU'LL HAVE TO KISS ME.
I-I...WHAT?
IT'S THE ONLY WAY TO CANCEL THE TRANSFORMATION. BE BRAVE, NOW!
TELL ME THIS ISN'T HAPPENING.

YUCK!
SMOOCH
POOOF
TA-DA! FROM TOAD TO ROCK STAR IN ONE EASY STEP. SEE? THAT'S MAGIC!
?!
DO YOU NEED ANOTHER KISS? I'LL VOLUNTEER!
NO NEED! I CAN FEEL THE INFUSION'S EFFECT WEARING OFF....
OOOOH!!
AH-HAH! THERE! BACK TO NORMAL!
NEVER MIND.
POOF
BE MORE CAREFUL NEXT TIME, YOUNG LADY! COLDS AND MAGIC DON'T PLAY WELL TOGETHER, AND... AAAAHH... AAAAHH...

AAAAAH...CHOOO!
AND MAGIC DEFINITELY DOESN'T KEEP COLDS AWAY!
SNIFF! CLASS IS FINISHED FOR TODAY! SNIFF!
BLOOM, YOU REALLY RAN YOURSELF RAGGED YESTERDAY! DID YOU FIND A JOB?
I WISH! SNIFF!
IT LOOKS LIKE NOBODY IN MAGIX NEEDS ANY HELP.
NO WAY!
PLENTY OF MY FRIENDS HAVE JOBS! IF THEY CAN GET HIRED, THEN YOU CAN TOO!

I DON'T KNOW... MAYBE I DON'T MAKE A GOOD FIRST IMPRESSION.
WELL... MAYBE YOUR *POWERS* COULD DO THAT! IF YOU WERE JUST A LITTLE *CUNNING*...
WHAT ARE YOU *SAYING*, STELLA? BLOOM IS A ***FAIRY***! SHE CAN'T ACT LIKE A... A ***WITCH***!
TECNA, I DIDN'T MEAN IT LIKE THAT!
GIRLS–NO NEED TO ARGUE! GUESS WHAT I FOUND ON THE ***ALFEA*** BULLETIN BOARD...
WHAT, FLORA?
IT'S A JOB AT ***WHITE HORSE***!
WHITE HORSE
I'M DOWN FOR ANYTHING AT THIS POINT. BUT WHAT'S ***WHITE HORSE?***
OH, IT'S A REALLY COOL LAKESIDE RESTAURANT JUST OUTSIDE TOWN!
IT'S SUPER POPULAR! INTERDIMENSIONAL TRAVELERS AND TOURISTS GO THERE, AND THERE'S EVEN A BEACH NEARBY.

BUT WHAT'S THE JOB?
WHO KNOWS? MAYBE THE RESTAURANT TURNS INTO A CLUB AT NIGHT, AND THEY'RE LOOKING FOR A *DJ!*
YOU'D TOTALLY MEET LOTS OF BOYS THAT WAY.
OKAYYYY.... WE'RE GETTING *OFF TOPIC* HERE.
BLOOM'S LOOKING FOR A JOB, NOT A BOYFRIEND! GET *SERIOUS!*
YOU'RE SURE SERIOUS! YOU ALMOST SOUND LIKE GRISELDA!
NEVER! ANYWAY... FLORA, WERE THERE ANY OTHER OTHER JOB POSTINGS?
NOPE, JUST THAT ONE FOR WHITE HORSE....
...AND I KNOW I SHOULDN'T HAVE DONE THIS, BUT I TOOK DOWN THE AD SO THAT NO ONE ELSE COULD REPLY BEFORE BLOOM!

AW! THANKS, FLORA!
NOW WHO'S ACTING LIKE A WITCH? I NEVER THOUGHT YOU'D DO SOMETHING LIKE THAT!
HEE HEE!
SOMETIMES, YOU GOTTA DO WHAT YOU GOTTA DO.
THAT'S MY PHILOSOPHY, TOO!
NOW IT'S UP TO YOU, BLOOM! I BET THIS JOB'LL BE THE PERFECT FIT FOR YOU.
LET'S HOPE SO!
SO WHEN DO YOU START WORKING, MUSA?
TODAY!
MISS BARBATEA CALLED THE SPECIALISTS IN TO HELP. I WONDER WHAT'S IN THAT ROOM?

THE NETWORK OF TUNNELS THAT EXTENDS UNDER ALFEA IS VERY LARGE AND COMPLEX. IT'S NEVER BEEN THOROUGHLY MAPPED OUT.
YOUR JOB IS TO VERIFY THAT THERE ARE NO DANGEROUS CREATURES LIVING UNDERNEATH THE SCHOOL. HOP TO IT!
YES, SIR!
I'LL GO IN THERE FIRST, ***BRANDON***. COVER ME!
GOT IT!

HI, MUSA! ER... TECNA'S NOT WITH YOU?
HI, TIMMY... NOPE, SHE'S STUDYING.
I'M HERE BECAUSE IT'S MY JOB... HEY, IS THAT A FRIEND OF YOURS?
WHO, RIVEN?
HE'S ONE OF THE SPECIALISTS! WANT ME TO INTRODUCE YOU?
OH, NO! I WAS JUST WONDERING, THAT'S ALL...
WELL, RIVEN'S A LITTLE STRANGE, ANYHOW. IT'S NOT EASY TO GET CLOSE TO HIM. EVEN I DON'T KNOW HIM ALL THAT WELL.
I BETTER GET GOING. SEE YOU LATER!
BYE! BE CAREFUL DOWN THERE!

THERE'S A STAIRCASE HERE. FOLLOW ME!

MEANWHILE...
THIS IS STOP 32.

WHITE HORSE IS RIGHT OVER THERE. YOU CAN'T MISS IT!
GREAT! THANKS AGAIN FOR YOUR HELP!

OH, WOW! LOOK AT THIS PLACE!

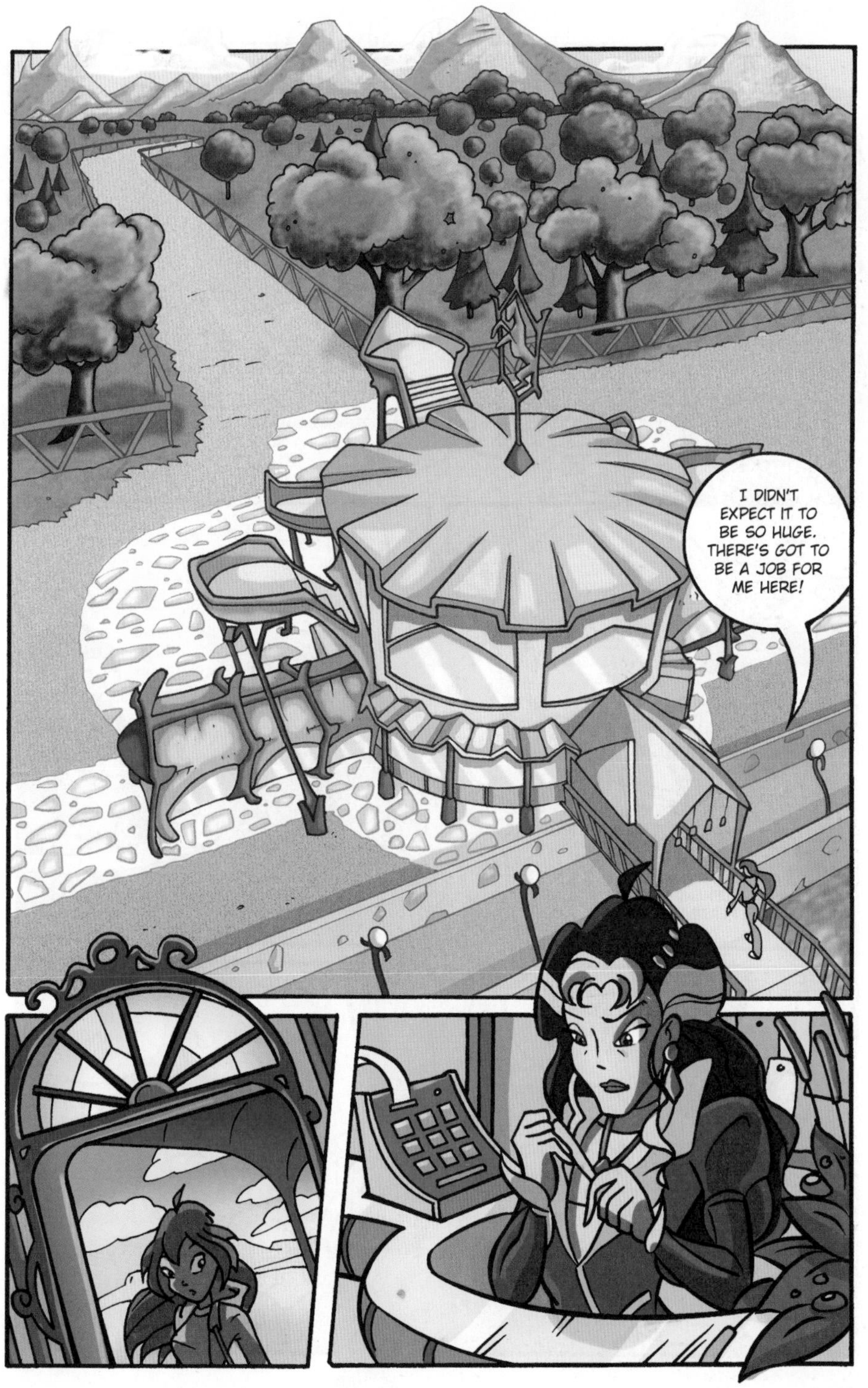
I DIDN'T EXPECT IT TO BE SO HUGE. THERE'S GOT TO BE A JOB FOR ME HERE!

GOOD MORNING! MY NAME'S BLOOM. I SAW YOUR AD ABOUT A JOB OPENING, AND I'D LIKE TO APPLY.
WONDERFUL! "BLOOM," YOU SAID? I'M MADAME GRETA, AND WE'RE LOOKING FOR WEEKEND WAITSTAFF.
IT'S ONLY ON WEEKENDS? THAT'S PERFECT FOR ME!
I SUPPOSE YOU DON'T WANT TO WORK MANY HOURS?
OH, I'M FINE WITH WORKING A LOT, MADAME GRETA! IT'S JUST THAT I NEED THE REST OF THE WEEK TO STUDY AND ATTEND CLASSES.
AH... YOU MUST BE A STUDENT AT THE FAIRY SCHOOL, HM?
ER... YES, I'M A FIRST-YEAR STUDENT AT ALFEA.
OH, ALFEA... I USED TO BE A FAIRY TOO, YOU KNOW, BUT THAT WAS MANY, MANY YEARS AGO.
REALLY? SO WHY DO YOU WORK HERE NOW?

BECAUSE I DIDN'T HAVE A CHOICE, YOUNG LADY! NOT EVERYONE CAN WASTE THEIR TIME ON THAT FOOLISH MAGIC YOU FAIRIES ARE SO PROUD OF.
HA HA! LOOK OUT! SHE'S ALLERGIC TO MAGIC—AND LOTS OF OTHER STUFF!
EEEP!
YOU HUSH UP! GO SERVE CUSTOMERS INSTEAD OF MEDDLING!
OKAY, OKAY! YES, MA'AM.
I'M SORRY IF I MADE YOU MAD! I DIDN'T MEAN TO UPSET YOU.
VERY WELL. I CAN TELL YOU DIDN'T MEAN ANY HARM.
NOW, THEN! TWO OTHER GIRLS ARE APPLYING FOR THE JOB TOO, SO I'LL HAVE TO SEE WHO'S BEST FOR IT.
OH!

BACK AT THE LIBRARY...
...SO, TIMMY? DID YOU GUYS FIND ANYTHING STRANGE?
NOT YET, MUSA. WE'RE STILL CHECKING THINGS OUT, ACTUALLY. IT'S AN UNBELIEVABLE MAZE DOWN THERE.
ANYWAY, HERE'RE SOME MORE BOOKS AND MANUSCRIPTS. THERE'S A TON OF THEM!
GRACIOUS, THEY'RE FILTHY! COULDN'T YOU HAVE CLEANED THEM FIRST?
GIVE ME STRENGTH! I DON'T KNOW HOW I'LL EVER DEAL WITH ALL OF THIS.
HOW ABOUT THIS? I'LL GO INSIDE AND CLEAN UP THE BOOKS BEFORE HANDING THEM OUT TO YOU GUYS. WE DON'T WANT MISS BARBATEA FALLING APART ON US!
PLUS, I'VE GOT A MAGIC SPELL I WANT TO TRY!

WHERE'S EVERYBODY ELSE?
OFF EXPLORING THE TUNNELS. I'M NOT SO SURE YOU SHOULD BE HERE, THOUGH. IT'S NOT SO SAFE...
OH, THERE'S NO REAL DANGER! BESIDES, I WANNA DO A GOOD JOB!
TURN MANY YEARS INTO A FEW... AND LET THESE BOOKS BE CLEAN AS NEW!
WHOA...!
THAT OUGHTA MAKE MISS BARBATEA HAPPY!
AMAZING! THEY PRACTICALLY LOOK BRAND NEW!
YOU REALLY CAN DO ANYTHING WITH MAGIC! WHAT DO YOU NEED US FOR?
TONS OF THINGS! MAGIC HAS ITS LIMITS.

I MEAN, MAGIC CAN'T DO *EVERYTHING*. BESIDES, IT TAKES LOTS OF CONCENTRATION AND ENERGY.
WE CAN'T USE MAGIC FOR TOO LONG WITHOUT GETTING EXHAUSTED. PLUS, THERE ARE THINGS IT JUST DOESN'T WORK ON. THAT'S WHERE YOU GUYS COME IN!
OH...
I'VE SEEN MAGIC BOUNCE RIGHT OFF SOME OBJECTS, AND *MONSTERS* CAN BE EXTRA RESISTANT.
Y-YEAH! WITHOUT US SPECIALISTS, YOU'D BE IN TROUBLE! HEH!
NOW, C'MON. STICK CLOSE BY. I'LL PROTECT YOU!
RIIIIGHT. HA HA HA!
WE SHOULD GRAB THAT TORCH. MORE LIGHT CAN'T HURT.
GOOD IDEA!
WHILE YOU'RE WORKING ON THE BOOKS, I'M GOING TO EXPLORE SOME MORE. THIS PLACE GOES ON FOREVER!

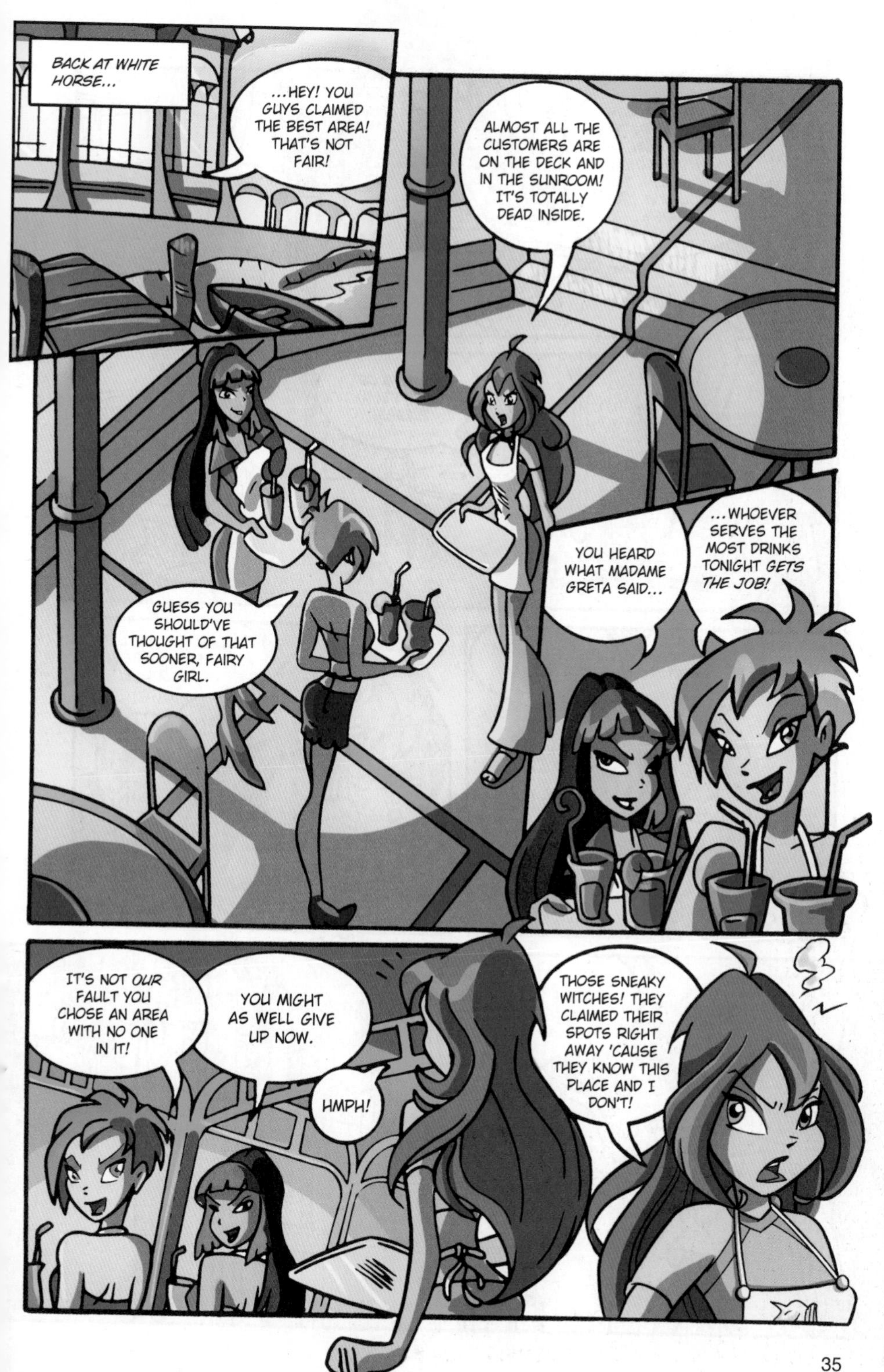
BACK AT WHITE HORSE...
...HEY! YOU GUYS CLAIMED THE BEST AREA! THAT'S NOT FAIR!
ALMOST ALL THE CUSTOMERS ARE ON THE DECK AND IN THE SUNROOM! IT'S TOTALLY DEAD INSIDE.
GUESS YOU SHOULD'VE THOUGHT OF THAT SOONER, FAIRY GIRL.
YOU HEARD WHAT MADAME GRETA SAID...
...WHOEVER SERVES THE MOST DRINKS TONIGHT *GETS THE JOB!*
IT'S NOT *OUR* FAULT YOU CHOSE AN AREA WITH NO ONE IN IT!
YOU MIGHT AS WELL GIVE UP NOW.
HMPH!
THOSE SNEAKY WITCHES! THEY CLAIMED THEIR SPOTS RIGHT AWAY 'CAUSE THEY KNOW THIS PLACE AND I DON'T!

BUT THEY'RE RIGHT. NO WAY I'M GETTING THIS JOB NOW, AND NOW I'M GONNA LOOK LIKE AN IDIOT. I SHOULD'VE TRIED HARDER...
A GLASS OF ROOT BEER, PLEASE!
RIGHT AWAY, SIR! WOULD YOU LIKE ANYTHING ELSE? OUR SANDWICHES ARE AMAZING, AND YOU COULD HAVE COFFEE AFTER DINNER...
JUST THE ROOT BEER, THANKS!
YOU GOT IT! IT'LL BE THE BEST ROOT BEER OF YOUR LIFE!
?!
A ROOT BEER FOR TABLE 26!

MY BONES ARE SO ACHY TODAY! FIRST THE RAIN, NOW THE TERRIBLE HUMIDITY...
WHAT IF WE ADJUST THE AIR CONDITIONING? YOU'D FEEL BETTER IF THE AIR WERE DRIER.
MAYBE SO, BUT...
...IT'S SUCH A COMPLICATED SYSTEM, I CAN'T MAKE HEADS OR TAILS OF IT. ONLY ONE EMPLOYEE KNEW HOW TO WORK IT, AND HE'S NOT HERE!
REALLY...
I CAN GIVE IT A SHOT! I ALWAYS ADJUSTED THE AIR FOR THE GREENHOUSES AT MY MOM'S FLOWER SHOP.
I'LL RUN THIS DRINK OVER TO THE CUSTOMER AND GET TO IT RIGHT AWAY!
HERE YOU GO–ONE FABULOUS ROOT BEER!

EMPLOYEES ONLY
THE A/C CONTROLS ARE PROBABLY IN HERE.
BINGO! NOW, THEN... TEMPERATURE... RELATIVE HUMIDITY...
THAT SHOULD DO IT! IT WASN'T SET PROPERLY, THAT'S ALL.
ALL DONE, MADAME GRETA! YOU'LL BE FEELING BETTER IN NO TIME AT ALL.
I HOPE YOU'RE RIGHT, DEARIE!
WHAT A BRIGHT LITTLE THING! SHE'S SO MUCH LIKE HOW I USED TO BE...
UGH, I'M EXHAUSTED! I THINK I OVERDID IT...

WHOOSH
?
OH, JUST PERFECT. THE TORCH IS OUT...
...AND I'M TOO WORN OUT TO RE-LIGHT IT WITH MAGIC!
TIMMY! TIMMY, WHERE ARE YOU?
TIMMY...?
ANRR R...
?!
QUIET!
MMPH?
SHH! WE'RE NOT ALONE DOWN HERE!
RRRR...

YOU'RE RIVEN, RIGHT? WHAT'S GOING ON?
KEEP YOUR VOICE DOWN.
STRANGE, AWFUL THINGS EXIST DEEP UNDER MAGIX. IT'S OUR JOB TO HUNT THEM DOWN AND FIGHT THEM...
ROWWRRRR...
...BUT SOME-TIMES THEY'RE TOO BIG TO HANDLE!
EW, DO YOU SMELL THAT? WHAT IS THAT?
A GIANT SERPENT-RAT, I THINK. LUCKILY, HE DIDN'T SMELL US.
HEY, DO YOU REMEMBER ME? FROM THE PARTY ...?
YOU DON'T LOOK FAMILIAR.
WELL, MY NAME'S MUSA. I'M A FIRST-YEAR ALFEA STUDENT. HOW ABOUT YOU?
I THINK WE CAN RISK A BIT OF LIGHT...

YOU DIDN'T ANSWER MY QUESTION.
ISN'T IT OBVIOUS? I'M TRAINING TO BE A SPECIALIST, AND I'M TRYING TO GET US SOME LIGHT!
YOU'RE CUTE, BUT ARE ALL YOU ALFEA FAIRIES SO CHATTY?
WHY ARE YOU BEING RUDE? I NEVER DID ANYTHING TO YOU!
I'M BEING RUDE? I CALLED YOU CUTE. YOU'RE OFFENDED BY THAT?
NO, BUT... LOOK, I'M SORRY.
I GUESS I MISUNDERSTOOD. I'M JUST TRYING TO BE FRIENDLY...
FRIENDLY? WHO NEEDS FRIENDS? THAT'S JUST A WORD FOR PEOPLE WHO CAN TAKE FROM YOU WITHOUT GIVING ANY-THING BACK!
I'LL ACCOMPANY YOU OUT AND THEN I'VE GOT TO REJOIN MY TEAM. I'VE BEEN DOWN HERE WAY TOO LONG.

MEANWHILE AT WHITE HORSE...
...MAN, THAT'S GOOD SODA.
THE BEST!
LET'S HAVE ANOTHER ROUND. HEY, MISS!
WHAT CAN I GET YOU?
ANOTHER ROUND FOR EVERYONE, AND MAKE IT NICE AND COLD!
I FEEL SO MUCH BETTER. BLOOM WAS RIGHT!
BUT GOODNESS, MY THROAT IS DRY. GET ME SOME WATER!
YOU'RE NOT THE ONLY ONE...
EVERYONE IN HERE IS A LOT THIRSTIER THAN USUAL.
FOUR ROOT BEERS FOR TABLE 18 AND THREE JUICES FOR TABLE 24!

HOLD ON A MOMENT. WHAT EXACTLY *DID* YOU DO TO THE AIR CONDITIONER?
ME? NOTHING!
I MADE THE AIR DRIER SO YOUR BONES WOULD ACHE LESS, THAT'S ALL.
OF COURSE, PEOPLE NEED TO DRINK MORE FLUIDS WHEN THE AIR'S DRY, BUT THAT'S NOT A PROBLEM, IS IT?
SO ***THAT'S*** WHY EVERYONE'S ORDERING MORE DRINKS?
WELL... IT'S WORKING, ISN'T IT??
GOOD POINT. I THINK I'VE SEEN ENOUGH. CALL ALL THE GIRLS OVER!
BLOOM WILL BE OUR NEW WAITRESS. SHE DID THE BEST JOB!
HOORAY!
WHAT?

THAT'S NOT FAIR! WE SOLD WAY MORE DRINKS THAN SHE DID!
LET ME TELL YOU TWO THINGS, YOUNG LADY...
ONE, I KNOW PERFECTLY WELL THAT THERE ARE MORE PEOPLE ON THE DECK AND UPSTAIRS. YOU HAD MORE CUSTOMERS, BUT BLOOM WORKED MUCH HARDER!
AND TWO, I MAKE THE DECISIONS HERE. CLEAR?
THE JOB IS YOURS, MY GIRL! I'LL SEE YOU NEXT WEEKEND.
THANK YOU SO MUCH!
YESSS! I DID IT! THIS IS ALMOST TOO GOOD TO BE TRUE!
I CAN'T WAIT TO TELL THE OTHERS!

NICE JOB, BLOOM! GOOD FOR YOU!
SEE? I KNEW YOU COULD DO IT!
AT LEAST ONE OF YOU HAD A GOOD DAY AT WORK...
WHAT DO YOU MEAN, STELLA?
MUSA'S REALLY BUMMED ABOUT SOMETHING. SHE WON'T COME OUT OF HER ROOM!
MUSA, WHAT HAPPENED?
I DON'T WANT TO TALK ABOUT IT.
C'MON, MUSA! WE'RE THE WINX CLUB, REMEMBER? LET IT ALL OUT SO WE CAN HELP YOU!
REMEMBER THAT GUY RIVEN? HE WAS AT THE LIBRARY TODAY, TOO.
I TRIED TO BE FRIENDLY TO HIM. BUT FIRST HE JUST IGNORED ME...

...AND THEN HE MADE FUN OF ME AND WALKED AWAY! LIKE I WASN'T EVEN THERE...
WHAT A HORRIBLE GUY!
YOU SHOULDN'T WASTE ANOTHER THOUGHT ON THAT...THAT...! HONESTLY, HE DOESN'T DESERVE YOUR TIME. FORGET HIM!
BUT I-
THERE ARE LOTS OF BETTER GUYS IN MAGIX. GUESS WHAT WE'RE GONNA DO?
WHAT?
WE'LL PLAN TO GO SOMEWHERE FUN THIS WEEKEND AND INVITE THE OTHER SPECIALISTS AND THEIR FRIENDS! IT'LL BE A BIG GROUP AND TONS OF FUN!
YEAH!
THIS WEEKEND? BUT...
YOU'LL FORGET ALL ABOUT THAT STUPID RIVEN! HOW'S THAT SOUND?
YEAH... LET'S TAKE A TRIP!
AWESOME, GUYS! I CAN'T WAIT!

THEY'LL ALL BE OFF HAVING FUN THIS WEEKEND, WHILE I HAVE TO WORK...
O-DAY, GIRLS! DA WEEK IS FINALLY OBER! HAB A NICE WEEKEND, EBERYBODY! SNIFF!
POOR PROFESSOR WIZGIZ STILL HAS THAT COLD...
TOO BAD FOR HIM, BUT SCHOOL'S DONE, FINALLY! COME ON, GIRLS!
LET'S GO GET READY FOR OUR TRIP! I'LL LET THE BOYS KNOW.
YAY! THE WEEKEND'S FINALLY HERE!
YEP... SIGH... IT'S HERE, ALL RIGHT...

GOOD MORNING, MADAME GRETA.
HELLO, DEARIE! YOU'RE THREE MINUTES LATE, SO RUN AND GET YOUR APRON.
IT'S YOUR OFFICIAL FIRST DAY, HUH? GOOD LUCK!
IT SEEMS YOU'RE THE SORT OF GIRL WHO MAKES LOTS OF FRIENDS. THAT'S LOVELY!
UM... THANK YOU?
TAKE THIS TRAY TO THE MAIN SEATING AREA. CUSTOMERS ARE WAITING!
YES, MA'AM!

?!
SURPRISE!
HA HA!
YOU'RE ALL HERE? BUT WEREN'T YOU–?
BE CAREFUL, BLOOM! PUT THAT TRAY DOWN!
DID YOU REALLY THINK WE FORGOT ABOUT YOU?
WE'RE HAVING OUR GET-TOGETHER RIGHT HERE BY THE LAKE. THAT WAY, WE CAN STILL ALL BE TOGETHER!

BESIDES, NONE OF US HAVE BEEN TO WHITE HORSE BEFORE!

YEAH, AND THIS PLACE IS AMAZING!

WE'LL HAVE TO COME HERE *REGULARLY!*

YOU DID THIS ALL FOR ME, STELLA... THANK YOU!

NO PROBLEM, KIDDO.

"AND THAT'S HOW WE ALL STARTED HANGING OUT AT WHITE HORSE. I DIDN'T REALIZE HOW BEAUTIFUL THE TERRACE AND THE DECK ON THE LAKE WERE 'TIL THEN..."

...BUT THE BEST PART WAS BEING REMINDED HOW GREAT MY FRIENDS ARE. IT WAS AMAZING TO SEE THEM ALL THERE—FOR ***ME!***

AND THE WEEKEND ISN'T EVEN OVER YET! WHO KNOWS WHAT ELSE MIGHT HAPPEN?

*THAT **IS** AMAZING! WE DIARIES HEAR A LOT OF STORIES, BUT THAT WAS ONE OF THE BEST ONES EVER.*

THE END

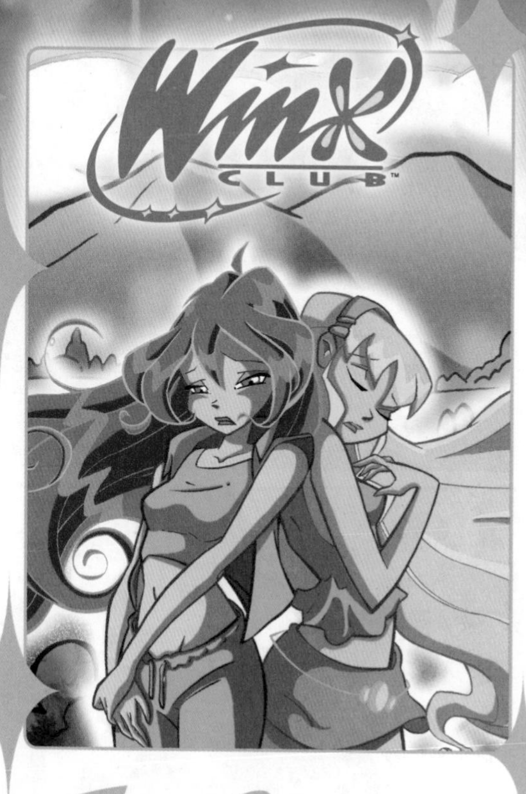

The Swamp Monster

A LOT OF THINGS LURK IN **BLACKMUD SWAMP**, BUT SOME THINGS ARE MORE DANGEROUS THAN OTHERS...

SQUAWK!

GROUAASSSHH

SQUAWK!

FOR NOW, THE WINX CLUB AND THEIR FRIENDS ARE SIMPLY ENJOYING EACH OTHER'S COMPANY AT WHITE HORSE...
IT'S SO AWESOME THAT YOU FOUND A JOB HERE, BLOOM. THIS PLACE IS AMAZING!
I KNOW! BUT IT'S A LOT OF WORK, AND I'VE BEEN SUPER TIRED LATELY.
DOES IT PAY WELL, AT LEAST?
NOT A LOT, BUT ENOUGH TO COVER MY EXPENSES. BESIDES, IT'S JUST A FEW HOURS EACH WEEKEND...
BYE, BLOOM! THIS WAS GREAT, BUT WE'VE GOTTA HEAD OUT!
ALREADY? OKAY...
HEY, SINCE YOU WORK HERE NOW, WE'LL BE BACK FOR SURE! SEE YOU SOON?
YEAH... REAL SOON!

MOM ALWAYS SAID A REGULAR JOB WOULD HELP WITH MAKING FRIENDS, AND I THINK SHE'S RIGHT!
WELL... IF *THAT* WAS ANY INDICATION, IT LOOKS LIKE YOU'RE DOING JUST *FINE*.
I SAW THAT GUY FLIRTING WITH YOU... SO ARE YOU *FRIENDS* NOW OR SOMETHING?
WHAT ARE YOU TALKING ABOUT, *SKY*?
EXCUSE ME?!
I WAS *BEING FRIENDLY!* CAN'T I TALK TO OTHER PEOPLE?
IT'S JUST THAT...
I'M JUST SAYING IT MUST BE GREAT TO MEET SO MANY GUYS WHILE WORKING HERE...
W-WELL, LOTS OF *GIRLS* COME HERE TOO, SKY! THIS IS A COOL SPOT, SO—

HMMM... SO YOU NOTICED THE *GIRLS* HERE, DID YOU, ***TIMMY***?
WELL, YEAH, ***TECNA***. I MEAN, NO. UH... WHAT I'M TRYING TO SAY IS THAT *EVERYONE* COMES HERE. IT'S NOT LIKE I'M, UH... *FLIRTING*...
OH, I GET THAT, TIMMY. 'CAUSE I'M NOTICING THE BOYS HERE, MYSELF.
YOU... YOU ARE?
UM... HEY, DID YOU KNOW TRAVELERS FROM OTHER DIMENSIONS COME HERE, TOO?
REALLY?
YUP! THEY TELL *GREAT* STORIES... SEE ***MUSA*** OUT THERE?
SHE'S BEEN GLUED TO HER SEAT LISTENING TO THOSE GUYS FOR AGES...!
AND THEN THESE *ALIENS* FIXED OUR *ENGINES*...

LOOKS LIKE THEY'RE HAVING FUN... ANYHOW, I BETTER GET BACK TO WORK...
SEE YOU LATER, BLOOM!
BYE!
BYE, SKY!
YEAH, SEE YOU...
MUSA, HAVE YOU SEEN STELLA?
I THINK SHE AND BRANDON ARE TAKING A WALK DOWN BY THE DOCK.
OH, MUSA'S RIGHT— I SEE THEM!
HEY, IT'S BLOOM OVER THERE! *HI!!!!*

AHH, IT'S *SUCH* A BEAUTIFUL WEEKEND! COMING TO THE LAKE WAS MY BEST IDEA EVER!
AND YOU REALLY PLANNED THIS TRIP BECAUSE BLOOM WORKS HERE?
YUP! HAVING A PART-TIME JOB MEANS SHE HAS LESS FREE TIME TO SPEND WITH HER FRIENDS NOW. AND SINCE THE ***WINX CLUB*** ALL PROMISED TO BE THERE FOR EACH OTHER...
...HERE WE ARE!!
"WINX CLUB, UNITE!" THAT'S YOUR *BATTLE CRY*, RIGHT?
HA HA HA! ***OW!*** I'M JUST TEASING, STELLA!
MAKING FUN, HUH? WELL, WE GIRLS ARE SERIOUS ABOUT THE WINX CLUB!
OW! OKAY! OKAY! THE WINX CLUB IS THE BEST!
I'LL SHOW YOU "BATTLE" ...!
OW! OW! I GIVE UP! I...
OH, WOW... AWESOME!

HUH? WHAT ARE YOU LOOKING AT?
THAT STRANGE-LOOKING OLD BOAT, BRANDON! ISN'T IT AMAZING?
ER... WHAT'S AMAZING ABOUT IT?
LOOK HOW BEAUTIFUL IT IS! I BET IT'S BEEN HERE FOR AGES.
IT'S NOT EVEN SEAWORTHY ANYMORE, BUT—OH!
HOW ROMANTIC! SOMEBODY CARVED THEIR INITIALS IN IT. G...PLUS M.

THEY WANTED TO RECORD THEIR LOVE FOREVER! EVEN IF NO ONE WILL EVER KNOW WHO THEY WERE...
DO YOU WANT ME TO CARVE OUR NAMES, TOO?
NO, NO! THIS IS THEIR OWN SPECIAL BOAT. IT WOULDN'T BE RIGHT TO PUT OUR MARK ON IT.
BUT IT'S SO SAD THAT IT'S TURNING TO DUST... TAKING THE MEMORY OF THEIR LOVE WITH IT...
I COULD FIX IT UP FOR YOU IF YOU WANT!
WHAT? *YOU* KNOW HOW TO FIX A BOAT?
I NEVER TOOK YOU FOR A "HANDYMAN" KIND OF GUY.
HEY, I'M GOOD AT A LOT OF THINGS! YOU JUST NEED TO GIVE ME A CHANCE TO SHOW YOU.
SO IT'S SETTLED. I'LL FIX THE BOAT FOR YOU!
OOH! WAIT 'TIL THE OTHERS HEAR ABOUT THIS!

I'M GOING TO FIND OUT WHO THE OWNER IS. WAIT FOR ME HERE, OKAY?
YOU GOT IT!
COME ON, MIRIEL. WE DON'T HAVE MUCH TIME LEFT.

OH, GIWIN!
I CAN'T DO THIS!
I CAN'T STAND
NOT BEING WITH
YOU!
IT'S NOT
FOREVER. YOU
KNOW THAT!

MY FATHER PROMISED
WE CAN BE TOGETHER
AGAIN AS SOON AS I
FINISH SCHOOL.
BUT ANYTHING
COULD HAPPEN IN
THE MEANTIME! AND
YOU'LL BE GONE SO
LONG...

HAVE FAITH IN ME!
I COULDN'T FORGET YOU
EVEN IF I TRIED.
THE TIME WILL FLY BY,
YOU'LL SEE...

...AND WHEN WE MEET
AGAIN, WE'LL BE TOGETHER
FOREVER! HERE, HOLD ON.

WHAT ARE YOU
DOING?
WE MET ON THIS
BOAT, REMEMBER?

THERE! NOW IT'LL
ALWAYS BE OURS.
FAREWELL,
MIRIEL.
GIWIN,
DON'T GO.
PLEASE...

I GOT THE GO-AHEAD, STELLA!
WHAT'S UP? ARE YOU OKAY?
I-I'M FINE. THERE'S JUST SOMETHING IN MY EYE.
UM... THERE, IT'S GONE.
THE OWNER OF THE DOCK SOLD THE BOAT TO ME, AND HE'S GOING TO SET UP A SPOT FOR ME TO WORK ON IT! ISN'T THAT PERFECT?
THAT'S FANTASTIC, BRANDON. THANK YOU FOR DOING THIS!
I'D DO THE IMPOSSIBLE FOR YOU, STELLA!
SO WHEN WILL YOU START WORKING ON IT?
WELL, IT'S TOO LATE TODAY, AND WE'RE BACK TO SCHOOL TOMORROW... I'LL GET CRACKING NEXT WEEKEND!

SCHOOL FOR THE SPECIALISTS WAS IN SESSION THE NEXT DAY, WITH A VERY IMPORTANT LESSON UNDERWAY...
AS YOU ALL KNOW, SOME INHABITANTS OF OUR UNIVERSE SUFFER FROM INTENSE NIGHTMARES CAUSED BY THEIR OWN PERSONAL TERRORS.
IN MOST CASES, THE NIGHTMARES FADE WHEN THE DREAMER WAKES. UNFORTUNATELY, SOMETIMES THIS FAILS TO HAPPEN.
OCCASIONALLY, NIGHTMARES SLIP INTO THE DREAM DIMENSION, THROUGH WHICH THEY ARE ABLE TO REACH MAGIX.
IT IS HERE THAT YOU MUST INTERCEPT AND NEUTRALIZE THEM, ENSURING THE SAFETY OF THIS ENTIRE WORLD!

TODAY'S PATROL WILL TAKE PLACE IN *BLACKMUD SWAMP!* IT'S EXACTLY THE SORT OF PLACE THAT CAN BRING SUCH FEARS TO LIFE...
...AND IT'S RIGHT BY THE LAKE, WHICH IS VERY POPULAR... MEANING THE DANGER'S GREATER. YOU'LL DEPART RIGHT AWAY.
SHOULD WE DIVIDE UP INTO GROUPS AS USUAL?
YES, AND BRING YOUR STANDARD EQUIPMENT. EACH GROUP WILL DEAL WITH ONE SECTOR.
A WHOLE SECTOR? BUT THAT'LL TAKE ALL DAY!
LET'S GO! THE SOONER WE START, THE BETTER!
I WISH IT WAS STILL THE WEEKEND. MONDAYS ARE WAY WORSE THAN MONSTERS!
HEY, *RIVEN*, TRY TO BE AT LEAST *KINDA* FRIENDLY ON THIS PATROL, OKAY? WOULDN'T WANT TO MISTAKE YOU FOR ONE OF THE *NIGHTMARES*.

UGH... ALL THESE TWIGS IN MY HAIR MAKE ME LOOK HORRIBLE! I HATE WALKING IN FRONT!
WHAT ABOUT ME, *ICY*? I'M THE ONE CARRYING THE BASKET OF STINKY HERBS!
WELL, DON'T DROP IT, ***STORMY!*** THIS IS—
I KNOW, I KNOW... THIS IS *IMPORTANT WITCH WORK.* AND ***DARCY'S*** DOING *NOTHING* TO *HELP* WITH IT!
HEY, I *FOUND* SOME OF THE RIGHT HERBS, DIDN'T I?
IF IT WERE UP TO *YOU* TO HARVEST FOR DARK MAGIC POTIONS, WE'D WIND UP WITH A *FLOWER BASKET* AND NO DARK MAGIC AT *ALL!*
HOW *DARE* YOU LECTURE ME! YOU THINK I'M STUPID OR SOMETHING...?

I'M SICK OF LISTENING TO YOU TWO BICKER! CUT IT OUT!
SHE STARTED IT!
NO, SHE DID!
SHUT UP OR I'LL MAKE YOU SHUT UP!
WE DON'T HAVE TIME FOR THIS NONSENSE! LET'S KEEP MOVING.
PICKING HERBS OUT HERE IS BORING ENOUGH WITHOUT LISTENING TO YOU TWO, SO LET'S FINISH THE JOB AND GO BACK TO CLOUDTOWER!
WAIT. I HEAR SOMETHING!

INTERESTING—THE SPECIALISTS FROM RED FOUNTAIN ARE HERE, TOO?
SHOULD WE HIDE?
THOSE BOYS ARE MORE INTERESTED IN ALFEA FAIRIES THAN CLOUD-TOWER WITCHES. THAT MAKES THEM STUPID, BUT... ALSO USEFUL.
WHAT ARE YOU GETTING AT, ICY?
WE'RE GOING TO GET THEM INTERESTED IN US!
FOLLOW ME!

AAH! OW!

WHO'S THERE?
?

M-MY ANKLE! IT HURTS SO MUCH!
WHAT? YOU DIDN'T EVEN ***TRIP!***

SHUT UP, YOU TWIT!

ARE YOU ALL RIGHT? CAN I HELP?

UNBELIEVABLE! LOOK AT THEM SWARMING AROUND HER!
HA! JEALOUS MUCH? YOU JUST WISH IT WAS YOU INSTEAD!

I CAN GET A BOY'S ATTENTION ANYTIME, UNLIKE *YOU!*
OH, YEAH? I'D LIKE TO SEE YOU *TRY!*

YOUR ANKLE SEEMS OKAY...
BUT IT HURTS SO BADLY! I CAN BARELY MOVE IT...

MAYBE IT'LL HELP IF WE WRAP IT IN SOMETHING. COME ON, WE'LL SIT YOU DOWN OVER THERE.

OUR POOR FRIEND REALLY DID A NUMBER ON HER ANKLE, BUT YOU DON'T SEEM TO CARE.
YOU WITCHES PROBABLY KNOW A DOZEN EASY CURES FOR A TWISTED ANKLE.
OH, IS THAT WHAT YOU THINK?
THE TRUTH IS, WE DON'T DEAL WITH SUCH TRIVIAL THINGS. WE USE OUR POWERS TO SOOTHE ENTIRELY DIFFERENT SORTS OF PAIN.
WE HAVEN'T BEEN INTRODUCED, HAVE WE? MY NAME'S ICY.
LIKE THE PAIN OF BEING UNLOVED... OR OF NOT BEING APPRECIATED PROPERLY FOR YOUR *TRUE WORTH*...
THERE YOU GO! HOW DOES THAT FEEL?
MUCH BETTER! YOU'VE BEEN SUCH A BIG HELP.

WAIT! WHAT DID YOU MEAN BY THAT—ABOUT BEING APPRECIATED FOR MY TRUE WORTH?
BECAUSE YOU DON'T THINK YOU *ARE*. RIGHT?
I-IT'S NOT LIKE THAT....
...WELL, MAYBE IT IS. BUT NO MAGIC POTION IS GOING TO CHANGE THAT!
IF THAT'S WHAT YOU THINK, THEN WE'RE DONE HERE.
WAIT!
TELL ME *MORE*...
OH!
...?!
BRANDON! SKY! GET OVER HERE, QUICK!

THAT'S **RIVEN!** C'MON, LET'S *MOVE!*

?!

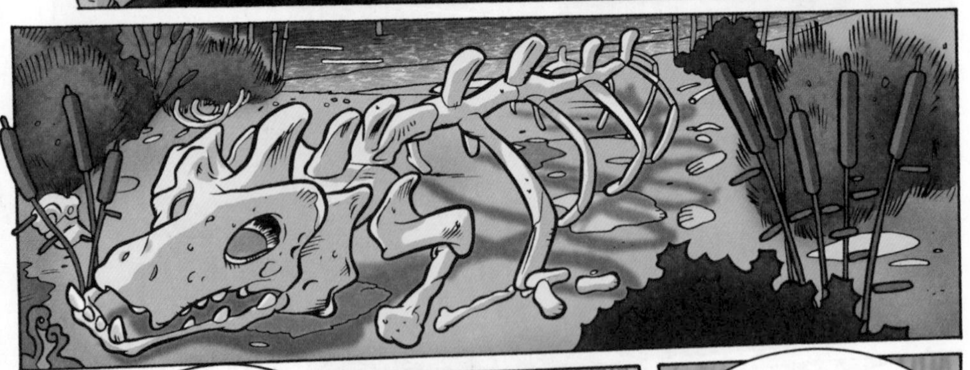

I DON'T KNOW OF ANY ANIMAL THAT'S CAPABLE OF SOMETHING ON THIS SCALE.
UH... MAYBE IT *WASN'T* AN ANIMAL.
I'D SAY THIS FITS OUR JOB DESCRIPTION! WE MAY BE DEALING WITH ONE OF THOSE **FEAR CREATURES**, SO STAY SHARP!
LOOK— I SEE *TRACKS*. LET'S FOLLOW THEM.
HEY, WHAT ABOUT US? ARE YOU GOING TO LEAVE US HERE ALL ALONE?
SHE'S RIGHT. I'LL STAY BEHIND TO KEEP THESE GIRLS COMPANY.
UH... YOU? KEEPING *ANYONE* COMPANY?
I'LL RADIO IF ANYTHING LOOKS SUSPICIOUS.

THESE TRACKS ARE FRESH, AND...
...LEADING TO A GROUP OF HIKERS!
UM, SORRY ABOUT MY GLASSES, GUYS. HEH....
THIS SWAMP IS SO CREEPY, BUT SO BEAUTIFUL...AND ITS NATURAL ENERGY IS AMAZING!
YEP—I CAN TOTALLY FEEL IT!
IS IT ENERGIZING YOUR POWERS, FLORA?
BRR... I THINK THE GROUND'S FEELING ME!
THAT HIKING GROUP—IT'S BLOOM AND HER FRIENDS!
WHAT? THEY'RE HERE, TOO?

HERE'S THE PERFECT MEDICINAL HERB FOR OUR POTIONOLOGY HOMEWORK. HELP ME PICK SOME!
HEY, CHECK IT OUT!
THERE'RE SOME FAMILIAR FACES OVER THERE, NO?
YOU'RE RIGHT! WHAT ARE THE SPECIALISTS DOING HERE?
NOT THAT WAY! TURN BACK!
THEY'RE IN THE MIDDLE OF ALL THOSE MONSTER TRACKS!
WHAT ARE THEY YELLING ABOUT?
I CAN'T MAKE SENSE OF IT.
THEY LOOK SCARED... MAYBE THEY'RE IN TROUBLE?
WHO KNOWS? JUST BOYS BEING SILLY, AS USUAL—
BLUOOB

GROUAAASSSCH
?!!
THAT THING'S ATTACKING THE GIRLS!
WEAPONS OUT! MOVE!!
SWISSSH
TUCK
SWOOOSSHHH

BZAZZZZ
SWOOOSSHH
ATTACK!!!
GET READY TO JUMP HIGH, WINX CLUB...
...BEFORE THIS THING PUNCHES US INTO A PUDDLE...
SGUOOSSH
...NOW !!!
TIME TO TRANSFORM! READY?

NOW!!!
FLASHHH
KRAAAKAZ
TECNA!
SGROOAASSSCH
AAAH!
RELAX, TIMMY! THAT THING HITS *HARD*...

...BUT I CAN HIT HARDER...
SSSSZACK
SLASH!
...AND CUT IT DOWN TO SIZE!
GROUAR-RRR!
IT'S GROWING NEW HANDS!!
SGUOOSHH
BUT WE'RE SLOWING IT DOWN! DON'T LET UP!
CURSES! THEY LEFT US STANDING HERE LIKE FOOLS!
JUST SO THEY COULD HELP THOSE STUPID ALFEA FAIRIES!
SO MUCH FOR YOUR TRICK, ICY. HOW'S YOUR ANKLE FEELING?
OH, SHUT UP! YOU THINK I'LL GIVE UP THAT EASILY?
WE'LL SHOW THOSE FAIRIES THAT THEY CAN'T TRUST THE BOYS TO PROTECT THEM..

YOU WANT TO HELP THAT MONSTER?
NOT EXACTLY. BUT IF WE SUMMON A STORM OVER THE WHOLE SWAMP, THEIR JOBS WILL BE THAT MUCH HARDER.
DOING THAT WOULD TAKE ALL OF OUR ENERGY. AND IF WE GET TOO TIRED, WE CAN'T DEFEND OURSELVES!
WHY WOULD WE USE OUR ENERGY, WHEN...
...WE'VE GOT A HERO RIGHT HERE?
A BRAVE BOY ITCHING TO FIGHT, HUH? HEE HEE!
THAT'S YOUR CUE, STORMY!
KRAKABOOM

KRAKABOOM

AGHHH!
WOSSHH

GROUAA!

I'M EXHAUSTED! CAN'T **STAY TRANS-FORMED...**

STAY BEHIND ME, TECNA!

GAH! HELP!
IT GOT TIMMY!
FOLLOW IT! DON'T LET IT ESCAPE!
KRAKTZ
BROOMMOOOMBROMM
PLIP PLIP PLIP
WE HAVE TO STOP THAT THING AND SAVE TIMMY!
I CAN'T SEE ANYTHING THROUGH THIS RAIN!

HA! NOW THIS IS MY IDEA OF FUN!
WE SHOULD STOP NOW. YOU'RE GOING TO REALLY HURT HIM!
A STRONG BOY LIKE HIM CAN HANDLE IT. NOW FOR THE BEST PART...
...A FLASH FLOOD!
LISTEN! WHAT'S THAT?
ROOA
GUASH
A TIDAL WAVE!
RAAAAAR
AAAH!
UP THERE! HURRY!
SGROUASSSH

SPLOOOSHH!!
THAT WAS CLOSE!
GRAB MY HAND!
WE'RE SAFE... BUT WHAT ABOUT TIMMY?
THE MONSTER'S GAINING POWER FROM THAT FLOOD SURGE...
...AND IT'S STILL GOT HIM!
WE'VE GOT TO SHUT IT DOWN WITH OUR MAGIC. GIVE ME A HAND, EVERYONE!

POWER OF SOLARIA!
...OF LINPHEA!
...OF MELODY!
...OF ZENITH!
BRAZZ
IT'S WORKING! WE'RE WEARING IT DOWN!
ZZRAZ
GLOGLOGLORSCH
OH, NO... I'M ALL OUT OF POWER...
BUT TIMMY'S FREE! WE JUST HAVE TO GRAB HIM!
I GOT HIM!

GIVE ME YOUR HAND!
NICE WORK, BRANDON!
COME ON, ALMOST THERE!
UP YOU GO!
OH, ALL RIGHT, I'LL HAVE STORMY STOP—IF YOU SAY, "PLEASE."
PLEASE, ICY!
OH, FINE...
I HOPE HE'S OKAY...
YOU'RE WORRIED ABOUT SOME STUPID BOY?
DON'T CALL HIM THAT! HE'S NOT LIKE THE OTHERS!
OH, CALM DOWN! WHY DO YOU CARE SO MUCH?

HE... COULD BECOME AN ALLY. THAT'S WHAT YOU WANT, ISN'T IT?
WELL, YEAH, BUT DON'T STRESS. HE'LL BE FINE, AND HE WON'T REMEMBER A THING.

IF YOU WANT TO STAY AND TAKE CARE OF HIM, *STAY*. WE'VE GOT *BETTER* THINGS TO DO!

TIMMY! TIMMY, ANSWER ME!
HE'S OUT COLD. WE HAVE TO GET HIM BACK TO RED FOUNTAIN AS SOON AS POSSIBLE!

THE WATER DESTROYED THE RADIO! WE'LL HAVE TO GO ON FOOT.
AND THE OTHERS?

AT LEAST SKY AND BLOOM ARE SAFE. I SEE THEM ON THAT ISLAND.

GUYS! WE'RE GOING TO GET HELP FOR TIMMY! WE'LL BE BACK FOR YOU SOON!
GOT IT!
LET'S GO! NO TIME TO WASTE!
CAN YOU FIND US A SAFE PATH, MUSA?
I'M ON IT.
THIS WAY! THE GROUND'S SOLID HERE!
OH...!

MY HEAD'S POUNDING! WHAT HAPPENED?
UM... LIGHTNING STRUCK NEARBY. IT'S AMAZING THAT WE SURVIVED.
I'VE NEVER FELT SO WEAK...
I'LL HELP YOU! JUST LEAN ON ME, OKAY?
ARE YOU OKAY, BLOOM? ANY INJURIES?
NO, BUT I'M FREEZING. MY CLOTHES ARE SOAKED...

TAKE MY CLOAK. IT'S WET TOO, BUT AT LEAST IT'LL BLOCK THE WIND.
THANKS!
I'VE NEVER SEEN SUCH A SUDDEN THUNDERSTORM. THAT MUST'VE BEEN WHY THE RIVER ROSE SO FAST.
I JUST HOPE TIMMY'S OKAY...
IT'LL BE A WHILE BEFORE BRANDON AND THE OTHERS GET HELP. WE SHOULD BUILD SHELTER AND TAKE COVER.
THERE! IT'S NO MASTER-PIECE, BUT IT'LL HELP SOME-WHAT.
I THINK IT'S GREAT!
BLOOM... I WAS ***MEAN*** TO YOU BACK AT WHITE HORSE...

...AND I'M SORRY.
APOLOGY ACCEPTED. BRR... NOW LET'S GET INSIDE AND MAKE A FIRE!
THIS WOOD IS SOAKED! MAYBE YOU CAN DO SOMETHING WITH YOUR MAGIC?
I DON'T KNOW, BUT I'LL TRY...
IT FIZZLED!
IT SEEMS A LITTLE DRIER NOW, AT LEAST.
I HAVE AN IDEA! MAYBE THIS BATTERY STILL HAS SOME CHARGE LEFT...
DO YOU HAVE A HAIRPIN?
YES!

HA! GREAT TEAM-WORK!
NOW, COME SHARE THIS CLOAK WITH ME.
ARE YOU FEELING BETTER?
YUP.
CAN WE MAKE UP THEN?

WUIIIINNN

THERE THEY ARE! THANK GOODNESS THEY'RE SAFE!

HELLO, SIR! WE'RE SURE GLAD TO SEE YOU.
SAME HERE, SKY. WE'VE BEEN LOOKING EVERYWHERE FOR YOU. NOW CLIMB IN, KIDS!
WE'RE HEADED HOME!
UIIiiiN NN

YOU'LL BE HAPPY TO HEAR THAT TIMMY'S FINE. HE GOT LUCKY TODAY. THAT SWAMP MONSTER IS ONE OF THE MOST DANGEROUS CREATURES IN MAGIX. IT'S AMAZING WHAT FEAR CAN CREATE!
I'M REALLY GLAD TIMMY'S OKAY. DID BRANDON FILL YOU IN ON EVERYTHING?
YES, HE DID. I HAVE TO CONGRATULATE YOU ALL ON A JOB WELL DONE. I'M SURE IT WAS A TOUGH ASSIGNMENT, BUT YOU NEUTRALIZED A BIG THREAT.
THE FAIRIES WERE A BIG HELP TOO, OF COURSE! GREAT TEAMWORK ALL AROUND.
WHAT AN EXCITING DAY! AND TO THINK WE WERE ONLY TAKING A LITTLE FIELD TRIP TO GATHER SOME FLOWERS!

BRANDON WAS INCREDIBLE! DID YOU SEE HOW HE JUMPED INTO THE WATER?
TIMMY WAS GREAT, TOO! HE SAVED ME FROM THE MONSTER IN THE NICK OF TIME. THANK GOODNESS WE'RE ALL OKAY!
AND WHAT ABOUT YOU, BLOOM? ALL ALONE ON THAT ISLAND WITH SKY? TELL ME ALL THE DETAILS!
OH, STELLA! NOTHING HAPPENED! WE'RE JUST BETTER FRIENDS NOW...
HOW ARE YOU, MUSA? THEY TOLD ME YOU SAW RIVEN...
YEAH, AND THAT WITCH DARCY WAS WITH HIM...
I FELT WEIRD AT THE TIME, BUT THEN THIS PRETTY STONE CAUGHT MY EYE. SOMETHING ABOUT IT REMINDED ME OF RIVEN, SO I PICKED IT UP. I'M GONNA KEEP IT AS A LUCKY CHARM.
I'M SURE RIVEN AND I WILL BE FRIENDS ONE DAY...
THE END

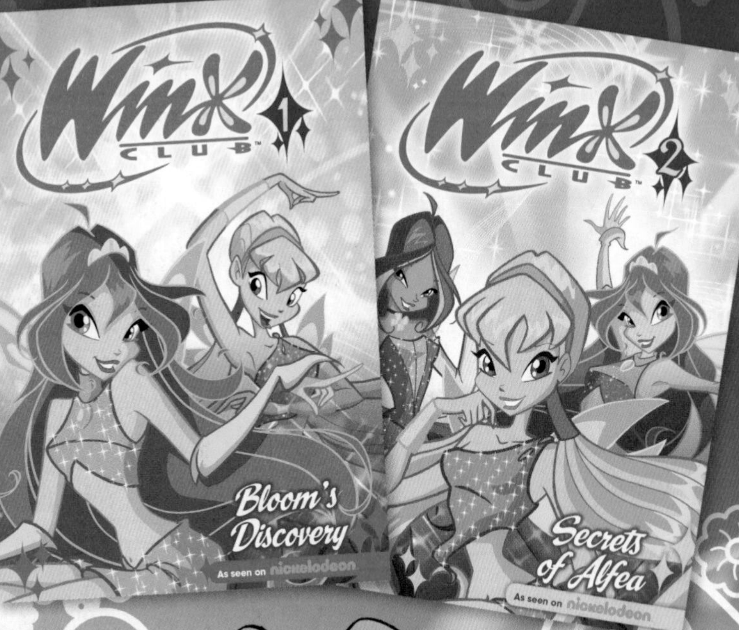

Look for MORE Winx Club Adventures

COMING SOON!